To Little George with love,
  ~Julia (aka Yuppie)

Herman Jiggle, Say Hello!

How to talk to people when your words get stuck

Written by
JULIA COOK

Illustrated by
Michael Garland

BOYS TOWN
Press

Boys Town, Nebraska

Herman Jiggle, Say Hello!
Text and Illustrations Copyright © 2020 by Father Flanagan's Boys' Home
ISBN 978-1-944882-51-8

Published by the Boys Town Press
13603 Flanagan Blvd.
Boys Town, NE 68010

For a Boys Town Press catalog, call **1-800-282-6657**
or visit our website: **BoysTownPress.org**

Publisher's Cataloging-in-Publication Data

Names: Cook, Julia, 1964- author. | Garland, Michael, 1952- illustrator.

Title: Herman Jiggle, say hello! : how to talk to people when your words get stuck / written by Julia Cook ; illustrated by Michael Garland.

Description: Boys Town, NE : Boys Town Press, [2020] | Series: Socially skilled kids. | Audience: Grades K-6. | Summary: All kids can relate to Herman Jiggle. He wants to make new friends, but he is so nervous his words get stuck. With practice and help from mom, he soon learns the important skills of introducing himself and starting a conversation.-- Publisher.

Identifiers: ISBN: 978-1-944882-51-8

Subjects: LCSH: Friendship in children--Juvenile fiction. | Interpersonal relations in children--Juvenile fiction. | Conversation--Juvenile fiction. | Public speaking--Juvenile fiction. | Oral communication--Juvenile fiction. | Anxiety in children--Juvenile fiction. | Stress in children--Juvenile fiction. | Success in children--Juvenile fiction. | Children--Life skills guides--Juvenile fiction. | CYAC: Friendship--Fiction. | Interpersonal relations--Fiction. | Conversation--Fiction. | Public speaking--Fiction. | Oral communication--Fiction. | Anxiety--Fiction. | Stress--Fiction. | Success--Fiction. | Conduct of life--Fiction. | BISAC: JUVENILE FICTION / Social Themes / Friendship. | JUVENILE FICTION / Social Themes / Self-Esteem & Self-Reliance. | JUVENILE FICTION / Social Themes / New Experience. | JUVENILE NONFICTION / Social Topics / Friendship. | EDUCATION / Counseling / General.

Classification: LCC: PZ7.C76982 H47 2020 | DDC: [E]--dc23

Printed in the United States
10 9 8 7 6 5 4 3 2 1

Boys Town Press is the publishing division of Boys Town, a national organization serving children and families.

My name is **Herman Jiggle.**
I don't like to talk to people very much…
especially people I don't know very well.

3

"Hello."

"Say 'Hello,' Herman."

"Hi, Hermie."

"Say 'Hi,' Herman."

*"Well Herman Jiggle,
how was your day?"*

"Tell him about your
day, Herman."

4

When I try to talk to people,
my tummy flips and then it flops
and then my words get tied in knots!
And they get stuck in my mouth right here.

SEE?

I'll just wave… it's a lot easier.

"Herman, when people say 'Hi' to you, you should say 'Hi' back."

"Why?"

"Because it's polite. Besides, that's how you're supposed to greet people and make a good impression."

"What's an impression?"

"It's what others think about you, and I want everyone in the whole wide world to know how wonderful you are."

"Why can't I just wave? It's easier."

"Sometimes waving works just fine. But most of the time, you should

LOOK at the person,

use your nice pleasant voice, and

say either 'Hi' or 'Hello.'"

7

"But Mom…
When I try to talk to people,
my tummy flips and then it flops
and then my words get tied in knots!
And they get stuck in my mouth right here.

SEE?"

"Well, of course they get stuck
because you forget to breathe
in deep before you talk."

"Breathe in through your nose before you speak,
then mix your words in with that air.
Open your mouth and say 'Hi' or 'Hello,'
and your words will shoot right out of there!"

"Okay, I'll try that tomorrow."

"Hello, Herman Jiggle."

"Hi, Hermie!"

"Hi, Herman. How was your day today?"

Just fine. Thank you.

"Herman, I'm so proud of you!
Your words just came right out!
Now try breathing in a little less air
because it isn't polite to shout."

"Okay, I'll try that tomorrow."

The next day at school, I said "Hi" back to everyone who said "Hi" to me, and I didn't even shout.

13

After school, my mom took me to the park to celebrate.

I saw a kid who was just like me playing just like I do and I really, **REALLY, REALLY** wanted to play with him.

"Go over there and introduce yourself, Herman."

"Mom, I don't even know what to say.
I don't even know how.
In fact, when I thought about talking to him,
I just about had a cow!!!"

"Well, you can start by saying,
'Hi. My name is Herman Jiggle. What's your name?'

And then when he tells you his name, ask him, *'Want to play?'*"

I slowly walked over to that boy, but when I opened my mouth…

My tummy flipped and then it flopped
and then my words got tied in knots!
And they got stuck in my mouth right here.

SEE?

I think I'll just wave… it's easier.

"Herman, you need to learn to introduce yourself to others and start up a conversation."

"Why?"

"That's how you make new friends. It will also help you make a good impression. And you know how I feel about good impressions. I want you to show the whole wide world how awesome you are!

Besides… it's polite."

"But Mom, just now when I opened my mouth…

My tummy flipped and then it flopped
and then my words got tied in knots!
And they got stuck in my mouth right here.

SEE?"

21

"Well, of course they got stuck in your mouth.
You forgot to smile big before you took your deep breath.

If you smile before you talk,
your body will start to relax.
Then your words will pour right out of your mouth
and not get stuck. It's a fact!"

"But what is there to smile about?"

"Think of something really funny. Imagine the person you want to talk to is standing in front of you, wearing polka-dotted jammies with chickens on them."

"Okay, I'll try that tomorrow."

The next day at school,
I introduced myself… to everyone!
And it was easy!

25

After that, it seemed like the more
I talked to others, the easier it became.

I talked…

And talked…

And talked…

Today my teacher gave me a special note to take home to my mom.

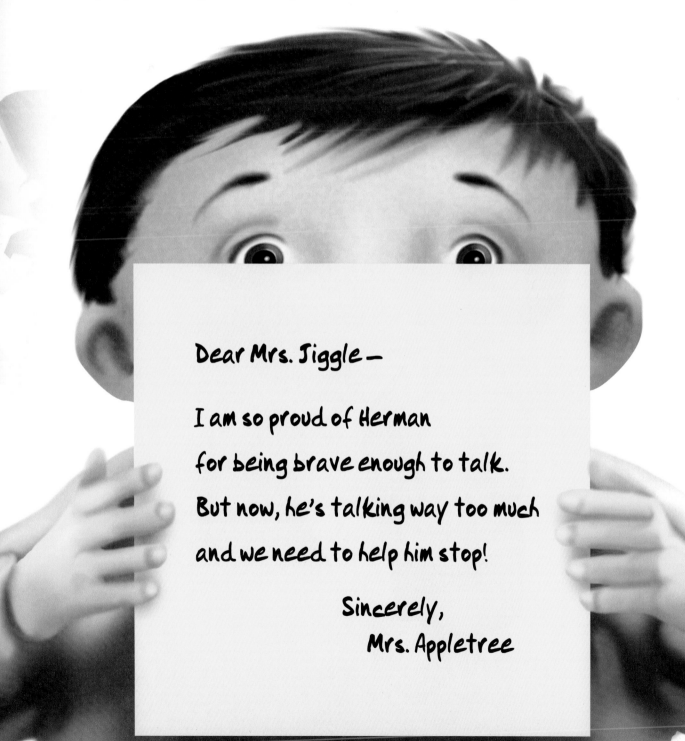

Dear Mrs. Jiggle —

I am so proud of Herman
for being brave enough to talk.
But now, he's talking way too much
and we need to help him stop!

Sincerely,
Mrs. Appletree

"Herman, I am really proud of you, too.
You have come SO far!
But there are times you should talk, and times you should not,
and you need to know when they are."

"Why?"

"So you can follow the rules. And it will help you make a good impression. And you know how I feel about good impressions. I want you to show the whole wide world how amazing you are!

Besides… it's polite."

"Okay, but can we work on
that tomorrow?"

"Sure."

Social anxiety is the fear of talking to, interacting with, and making friends with others. Children with social anxiety worry that others will see them in a negative way. Unfortunately, this fear can make it difficult or impossible for children to take risks and develop a growth mindset. It's often also the reason why children are afraid to fail. Helping your child overcome social anxiety can be a challenge. Here are some helpful tips that can get you started.

1. First, make sure your child feels he or she is being **SEEN, HEARD,** and **VALIDATED** by you. Talk through fears and validate feelings. For example, you can say something like, "I can only imagine how scary that must seem to you."

2. Explain anxiety, how it works, and why it is important. Everyone is supposed to have some anxiety. It keeps us on our toes and helps us stay out of danger. But when we have too much anxiety, it can take over how we think, feel, and behave. Decision-making strategies and feelings of anxiety are processed in the same region of the brain. Too much anxiety causes us to make poor decisions.

3. Prepare your child in advance. If you know a stressful situation is coming up, practice by role-playing the situation in a safe environment before it happens. Explore and discuss with your child possible scenarios that could occur. Prediction, practice, and preparation are huge when it comes to helping children deal with all forms of anxiety.

4. Focus on and celebrate your child's progress rather than always expecting perfection. Social anxiety is sometimes strongly associated with the need to be perfect. Teach your child the **Power of YET!**

That means helping him or her move from saying, "I can't do this," to saying, **"I can't do this YET."**

5. Try not to feed into the problem. If you appear worried or overly concerned when your child feels anxious, you will only increase his or her anxiety. Keep a matter-of- fact, encouraging, validating, proactive attitude, and keep your own emotions in check.

6. Teach basic skills like how to greet others, how to introduce oneself, and how to start up a conversation to set your child up for social success. Be sure to practice those skills with your child so the steps become familiar and easy to use when he or she does feel anxious.

7. **Set a good example.** Talk through your own social anxieties and explain to your child how you deal with them.

8. **Teach children to be the boss of their worries** and to not let their worries be the boss of THEM!

For more parenting information, visit **boystown.org/parenting**.

BOYS TOWN®
Saving Children Healing Families

Boys Town Press Books by Julia Cook

Kid-friendly titles to teach social skills

The Leader I'll Be! *series teaches children how to use collaboration, creativity, and compromise to influence others.*

It's My Way or the HIGHWAY
Turning Bossy into Flexible and Assertive
Written by Julia Cook
Illustrated by Kyle Merriman
978-1-944882-37-2

THE GREAT COMPROMISE
Illustrated by Kyle Merriman Written by Julia
978-1-944882-44-0

The LEADER I'll Be!

Responsible ME!

A book series that delivers a powerful message about accountability and honesty.

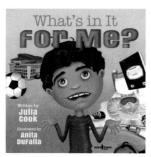
What's in It For Me?
Written by Julia Cook
Illustrated by Anita DuFalla
978-1-944882-30-3

OTHER TITLES: Baditude!, The PROcrastinator

But It's Not My Fault
Written by Julia Cook
Illustrated by Anita DuFalla
978-1-934490-80-8

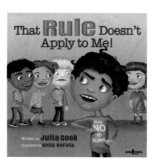
That Rule Doesn't Apply to Me!
Written by Julia Cook
Illustrated by Anita DuFalla
978-1-934490-98-3

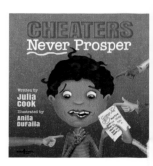
CHEATERS Never Prosper
Written by Julia Cook
Illustrated by Anita DuFalla
978-1-944882-08-2

UNIQUELY WIRED!
A Story about Autism and Its Gifts
Written by Julia Cook
Illustrated by Anita DuFalla

RUMOR HAS IT...
Illustrated by Kyle Merriman Written by Julia Cook

Building RELATIONSHIPS

A book series to help kids get along.

Making Friends Is an Art!
Cliques Just Don't Make Cents
Tease Monster
Peer Pressure Gauge
Hygiene...You Stink!
I Want to Be the Only Dog
The Judgmental Flower
Table Talk
Rumor Has It...

COMMUNICATE with Confidence

A book series to help kids master the art of communicating.

Well, I Can Top That!
Decibella
Gas Happens!
The Technology Tail

BEST ME! I Can Be

Winner of the Mom's Choice Award!

The Worst Day of My Life Ever!
el PEOR día de TODA mi vida
I Just Don't Like the Sound of NO!
¡No me gusta cómo se oye NO!
Sorry, I Forgot to Ask!
I Just Want to Do It My Way!
Teamwork Isn't My Thing, and
I Don't Like to Share!
Thanks for the Feedback... (I Think!)
I Can't Believe You Said That!

BOYS TOWN Press
BoysTownPress.org

For information on Boys Town, its Education Model®, Common Sense Parenting®, and training programs:
boystowntraining.org | boystown.org/parenting
training@BoysTown.org | 1-800-545-5771

For parenting and educational books and other resources:
BoysTownPress.org
btpress@BoysTown.org | 1-800-282-6657